Five on the Bed

BY ADDIE BOSWELL

WEST MARGIN PRESS

There is
ONE
on the
bed.

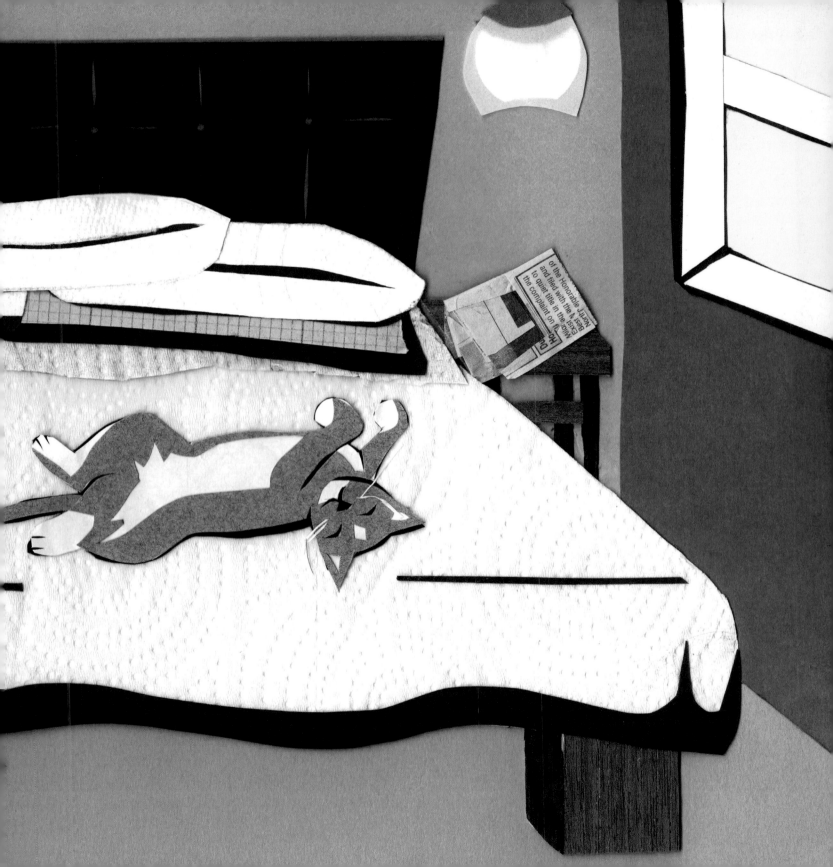

ONE on the bed and

ONE below the bed.

Now
there
are
TWO.

explodes into the colorful
e park is famous, but also
side. In a tent. The first
ad pitched a tent was the
ny living room, holding a
my husband did most of
We sustained
ter we got o
irst cactus injury righ
the car. My 10-year-o
judgment will be taken against

TWO
on the bed
and
TWO
below.

FOUR
on the bed!

THREE

off

the bed

and
ONE
above!

Now
there are
NONE
on the
bed.

coated s
top | $500 at Uhuru
uhurudesign.com

■ Is the weight important? Yes, a
should be robust enough that it do
Mr. Dorsey said, but light enough t
move between rooms.

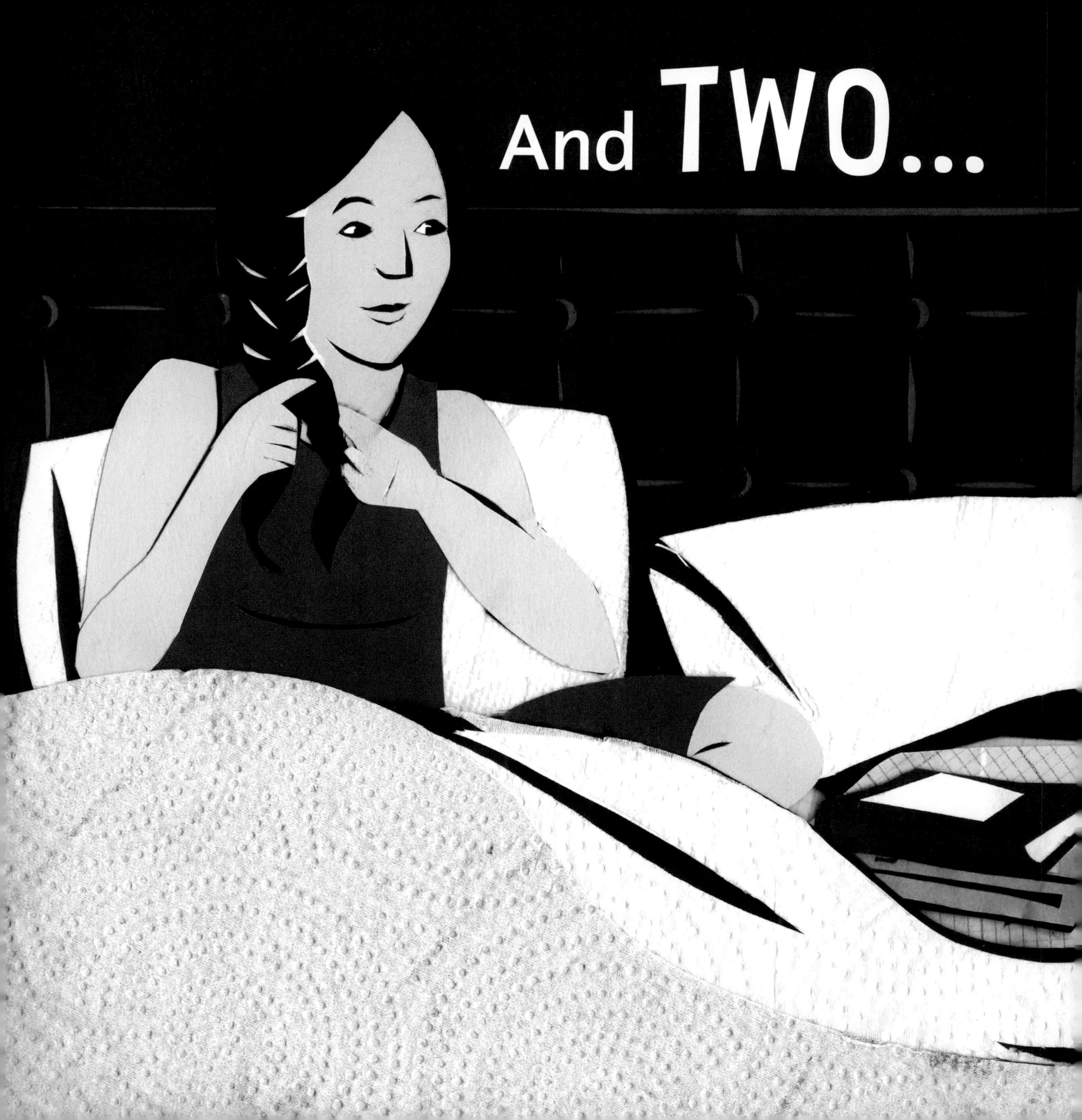
And TWO...

and
THREE...

and FOUR...

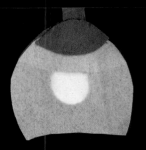

FIVE
ON THE—

Shhhh...

FIVE on the bed, fast asleep.

Dedicated to my four: Adam, Immie, Beazle, and Cucamonga.

Text & Illustrations © 2020 by Addie Boswell

Edited by Michelle McCann

All rights reserved. No part of this book may be reproduced
or transmitted in any form or by any means, electronic or
mechanical, including photocopying, recording, or by any
information storage and retrieval system, without written
permission of the publisher.

Library of Congress Cataloging-in-Publication Data

Names: Boswell, Addie K., author, illustrator.
Title: Five on the bed / Addie Boswell
Description: [Berkeley] : West Margin Press, [2020] | Audience:
    Ages 3. | Audience: Grades K–1. | Summary: A young girl, her
    parents, and their dog and cat appear on, under, and next to
    the bed as they all get ready to sleep in this counting book
    featuring cut paper illustrations.
Identifiers: LCCN 2020018749 (print) |
    LCCN 2020018750 (ebook) | ISBN 9781513264288 (hardback)
    | ISBN 9781513264295 (ebook)
Subjects: CYAC: Family life—Fiction. | Bedtime—Fiction. |
    Beds—Fiction. | Cats—Fiction. | Dogs—Fiction. | Counting.
Classification: LCC PZ7.B65125 Fiv 2020 (print) |
    LCC PZ7.B65125 (ebook) | DDC [E]—dc23
LC record available at https://lccn.loc.gov/2020018749
LC ebook record available at
    https://lccn.loc.gov/2020018750

Proudly distributed by Ingram Publisher Services

Printed in China
24 23 22 21 20 1 2 3 4 5

Published by West Margin Press

WEST
MARGIN
PRESS

WestMarginPress.com

WEST MARGIN PRESS
Publishing Director: Jennifer Newens
Marketing Manager: Angela Zbornik
Project Specialist: Gabrielle Maudiere
Editor: Olivia Ngai
Design & Production: Rachel Lopez Metzger